MINI SAGAS
THE ADVENTURE STARTS HERE ...

THE MIDLANDS

First published in Great Britain in 2008 by
Young Writers, Remus House, Coltsfoot Drive,
Peterborough, PE2 9JX
Tel (01733) 890066 Fax (01733) 313524
All Rights Reserved

© Copyright Contributors 2008
SB ISBN 978-1-84431-912-1

Disclaimer
Young Writers has maintained every effort
to publish stories that will not cause offence.
Any stories, events or activities relating to individuals
should be read as fictional pieces and not construed
as real-life character portrayal.

FOREWORD

Since Young Writers was established in 1990, our aim has been to promote and encourage written creativity amongst children and young adults. By giving aspiring young authors the chance to be published, Young Writers effectively nurtures the creative talents of the next generation, allowing their confidence and writing ability to grow.

With our latest fun competition, *The Adventure Starts Here...*, primary school children nationwide were given the tricky challenge of writing a story with a beginning, middle and an end in just fifty words.

The diverse and imaginative range of entries made the selection process a difficult but enjoyable task with stories chosen on the basis of style, expression, flair and technical skill. A fascinating glimpse into the imaginations of the future, we hope you will agree that this entertaining collection is one that will amuse and inspire the whole family.

CONTENTS

THE MINI SAGAS

THE CREEPER

The hairs on the back of my neck were standing
up straight with fear. Something was in the house,
I could feel it. I edged towards the door, then it
appeared from upstairs. A horrible fanged creature.
It was upon me so quickly.

ZAK BENTLEY (10)

Abbey Primary School, Walsall

1970S ITALIAN JOB

Charlie comes out of prison and robs a bank of four million dollars in gold, using three special Mini Coopers as getaway vehicles. Will they get away scot-free or will it be a prison job instead of an Italian job?

ALEX RUDGE (11)

Abbey Primary School, Walsall

A DAY OUT

One morning I went for a picnic at this park with my mum and dad. I got lost, I was terribly worried so I walked back to the car and my parents were only sitting on a bench eating their lunch. They didn't even notice that I had gone missing!

JESSICA BUCKINGHAM (11)
Abbey Primary School, Walsall

THE GHOST WHO HAUNTS CHINA TOWN

A dark gloomy night. A man walking his dog, that
night, the chain loosened, the dog ran off out of sight.
The man ran after the dog, when suddenly, he saw
something glowing. It got colder and shivering.
The thing came out from hiding, it was a ghost.

RYAN HIGGINS (11)
Abbey Primary School, Walsall

HEAD SHOT

Bang! A gun was fired in a shop by a robber. He said,
'Give me the money!'
The terrified cashier said, 'No, go away.'
Eventually the cashier gave him the money because
he threatened to shoot him. He put the gun to his
head and said, '1, 2 ...' then he fired.

SEAN BARNARD (11)

Abbey Primary School, Walsall

DARK, DARK

In a dark, dark house, down dark, dark stairs,
in a dark, dark hall, in the dark cellar, some skeletons
lived. A dog skeleton, a middle skeleton and a big
skeleton who liked to scare people. One dark night,
they went out to play on the swing for some fun.

PAUL HANNON (11)
Abbey Primary School, Walsall

6

AIR BUD

Seven dogs mess the house up by pulling cotton wool everywhere. The puppies went out for a walk on their own. Two men grabbed them and took them away. But their mum and dad knew something was wrong, so they went to the police dog and he found them.

LAUREN SPOONER (11)

Abbey Primary School, Walsall

BONES

'Run!' they all screamed. The Earth shook as bones
raised from the graves of the underworld.
They joined together making a monster out of bones
that other people left behind. Screaming in terror,
the five children carried on running, but now for
their lives. That was the end …

NICOLE BENTLEY (11)

Abbey Primary School, Walsall

ROCK 'N' ROLL

The butterflies came into his belly. He came on stage with his guitar and performed songs like 'Two Minutes to Midnight', and 'Paranoid'. He was relieved to go home. He had a long tour around the USA. He and Zippy, aka the drummer, went home and played some more.

THOMAS PEARCE (11)

Abbey Primary School, Walsall

9

IT'S ONLY A HAIRCUT

I opened my door to see if there was anything going on. My heart was pounding. I heard a laugh and metal clashing and clicking. I took a breath and said to myself, *this is it!* I walked in, saying 'Spare me!' Mum said, 'You're only having a haircut!'

SHOUKAT HUSSAIN (11)

Ashfield Park Primary School, Ross-on-Wye

THE FOOTBALL MATCH

There I was at the biggest match in the world,
England vs Croatia in the World Cup Finals. It was
the last minute and it was 1-1. England had a corner,
they crossed it and it went flying in! The crowds
erupted.
It went quiet, it had been disallowed.

LEWIS JONES (11)

Ashfield Park Primary School, Ross-on-Wye

11

THE BATTLE

The mercenaries stood soundlessly waiting for a command on the rough ground. The commander shouted, 'Have no mercy, leave no prisoners. Attack!' Swords clashed, axes lopped off heads.
They fought for weeks on end, they received heavy casualties on both sides. This was the end for the enemy mercenaries.

MATTHEW FALLON (11)

Ashfield Park Primary School, Ross-on-Wye

THE DARKNESS

I was led down silently in darkness. As I turned my head, I saw long strands of grass waving at me in the wind. Suddenly the sky lit up. I saw a shooting star flying towards the moon that was pulsing like a heart. The star hit the moon. *Bang!*

TARA SAUNDERS (10)
Ashfield Park Primary School, Ross-on-Wye

GHOST

My head turned slowly around. There was a shadow,
it was moving. It looked like a tree, with witches'
fingers reaching out. It was moving towards me. It
was a ghost haunting the room. It came closer. *Bang!*
Right in my face. I'm gone.
I'm the ghost haunting the room.

CHLOE BLOMFIELD (11)

Ashfield Park Primary School, Ross-on-Wye

SATS PAPER

As I sat down, the maths paper stared at me. I picked
up my pen, the teacher said, 'You may start.'
I slowly opened my first page, then the door opened,
my mum walked in and said, 'Stop we're going
to Florida!'
'Wake up Charley, you're late for school!'

CHARLOTTE PRINCE (11)
Ashfield Park Primary School, Ross-on-Wye

MYSTERIOUS MIDNIGHT

The midnight shadows were glowing down on the
trees, which were like long, skinny fingers.
The moonlight shining down, scattering almost like
a thousand mirrors spreading it. The lake shimmered
under the moonlit sky.
I heard an ear-piercing scream.
'Did you have another nightmare Rosie?'
'Argh! Oh yeah Mum!'

EMMA HAZELWOOD (11)
Ashfield Park Primary School, Ross-on-Wye

THE FUTURE EARTH

The sky was orange, however, not a nice orange, but
a polluted orange - cloudy and misty. Brown trees
stood ridged as statues, dead as squished flies.
The grey ground was hard and cracked underfoot as
I walked through the sweltering heat. I stopped;
a thought struck me: Where was everyone?

JANE MCNAMARA (11)
Cheswardine Primary School, Market Drayton

17

FALLING

I was strolling through a forest when I saw a glint in the distance. I ran towards it, suddenly trees started falling. It felt like the whole world was falling. I bolted down the treacherous path that led this way and that. Every tree was collapsing. I was trapped.

EMILY JONES (11)
Cheswardine Primary School, Market Drayton

DAY AT THE BEACH

One sweltering day I was on a beach down south.
I was bored so I started kicking sand. Just then,
I kicked something. I took my spade out and started
to dig. The first time I tried, my spade broke.
What I thought was treasure, was only a shiny rock!

DANIEL ASH (10)

Cheswardine Primary School, Market Drayton

THE SCARY NIGHT

As Alice was lying in her bed, she heard a noise that sounded like this. *Tick-tock*. She thought it was only the clock, so she went back to sleep but all of a sudden, the door opened and somebody grabbed her, nobody ever saw Alice ever again.

ABBIE MITCHELL (11)

Cheswardine Primary School, Market Drayton

THE SEA MONSTER

Suddenly the powerful wave struck, my puny boat had completely collapsed. All of a sudden, in the blink of an eye, the boat sunk. There was something there. Unexpectedly a monster jumped up in a rampage. It had large feet, a large head and long arms. What could I do?

ANDERS JENSEN (10)

Cheswardine Primary School, Market Drayton

TREASURE GALORE

Once a pirate called Jimmy went on a massive ship to find some treasure. He got to the island and found the X. He started digging and he still couldn't find it. He stayed the night, then sometime in the middle of the afternoon, he found it and returned rich.

FRANCIS CROCKER (10)
Cheswardine Primary School, Market Drayton

THE HARBOUR GATES

I drove in on the night of Friday the 13th.
The harbour gates were closed. The darkness filled
the air that night and what happened, nobody knows.
I thought the gates would open, my heart pounding
straight. Then I remembered the captain had died, a
ghost was out.

BRETT TWIST (10)

Cheswardine Primary School, Market Drayton

I WONDER

Running as fast as I could, through the dark deep
woods, I wondered if I could ever make it through.
I started to shiver as I ran faster. Cold sweat dripped
off my face as I fell to the ground.

LUCY BAXBY (11)
Cheswardine Primary School, Market Drayton

THE LEGENDARY

I walked down the lane, I heard the citizens talking about the legend of Gold Horn. It's meant to call dragons. I searched and searched everywhere apart from the hoods. I searched hard. *Bump!* I hit something cold, shiny and small; a box. Could it be the legendary, Gold Horn?

BRIAR CASEY (10)

Cheswardine Primary School, Market Drayton

THE NIGHTMARE EXPERIENCE

I was walking home through the park, only a lantern lit the dark night. Then I stopped and listened, there was a strange humming noise. It grew louder, a screaming, clattering noise, then with blinding light, a train came whizzing past, sparks jumping from the wires. Then it was gone.

MATTHEW RICHARDS (11)

Cheswardine Primary School, Market Drayton

UNTITLED

James was swimming in the sea and hit a jellyfish, it stung him. James struggled to get out of the sea but couldn't. He was in pain, 'Help!' he called out, 'Help!' Along came a sailor who helped him get out of the sea and took him home.

RACHEL WATLING (10)

Cheswardine Primary School, Market Drayton

THE STRANGER

One day a little girl was playing in her garden with her football, when suddenly a strange man grabbed her and ran off with her. She was screaming, 'Help,' but nobody could hear her.

EMILY THACKER (11)

Cheswardine Primary School, Market Drayton

GLORIOUS BEACH

As I came down the steep rocky steps, the golden sun was shining down on the sand. Children were building sandcastles, adults were sunbathing. I made my way to the sea, sand in my toes. I plunged into the sea, glistening water all around me.

RACHAEL OWEN (11)

Cheswardine Primary School, Market Drayton

A DISASTER AT THE MUSEUM

One day I was at the Myths and Legends museum where there are statues that had been alive millions of years ago. Suddenly, one of the statues started to blink and move. I ran out into the cold air, I was safe now, but did anybody else get out?

NATASHA TIPTON (10)

Cheswardine Primary School, Market Drayton

BILL'S SPORTS DAY

Bill was rubbish at sport, skipping was too hard. His clumsy feet spoilt running, but Sport's Day was coming up at Flower School. Miss Honey had chosen him for tug-of-war. On Sport's Day, he was very nervous. He pulled and pulled and his team won! They had cookies.

KRISTINA BLANK (8)

Cheswardine Primary School, Market Drayton

THE CURSE

Once upon a time there was a dragon who lived in a
cave. There was a prince under a curse. He had been
cursed so he could not talk. He had a special mike
so he could talk. He said he would go and slay the
dragon and he did.

TOM HOLDEN (8)

Cheswardine Primary School, Market Drayton

LITTLE RED RIDING HOOD

One day a little girl called Red went in the woods to
see her sick granny but when she got there, she had
a big shock. Her gran had big teeth. 'Granny?'
'Yes,' said the fox. 'Come in.'
Roar! Red got a gun and shot him. *Bang! Yay!*

LEAONIE RAWLINGS (9)

Cheswardine Primary School, Market Drayton

THE MOONEIGH

In the olden days there were tons and tons of myths and legends but I am going to focus on just one of them. We are going to be focusing on the Mooneigh. The Mooneigh was half cow and half horse, that is how it got its name, moo neigh.

TYLER CASEY (8)

Cheswardine Primary School, Market Drayton

THE MOONLIGHT

One night a little round moon up in the dark, black sky was sparkling down on the ground and it shone with power. A black bat flew across the moon. The wind blew a cloud over the moon, it went very, very dark and gloomy. *Argh!*

ELEANOR BROWN (8)

Cheswardine Primary School, Market Drayton

ESCAPING THE HUTCH!

One night in the mist of darkness, Sandy the mysterious rabbit got loose by thumping her hutch door open. She hopped out with a tiny bounce and began her adventure. She bounced over to where the compost bin was sitting and started pulling up clumps of rhubarb … crunch, crunch, crunch!

KATIE FERGUSSON (9)

Edge Hill Junior School, Burton-Upon-Trent

IT'S ALIVE!

It was a cold, gloomy night as Professor Brainstorm
sat in his laboratory. He cackled at the monstrosity
he had created. The professor slipped a foul green
glowing test tube out of his pocket and poured the
mixture over the body. It stirred and woke.
This terrifying creature was alive!

JESSICA BRASSINGTON (9)

Edge Hill Junior School, Burton-Upon-Trent

LAVA MONSTER ATTACKS!

I was hiking near a volcano when suddenly a gigantic
explosion happened and a large lava monster leapt
out. I was so scared, I cried huge tears onto the
monster and it melted. The volcano exploded again
and the noise woke me up. It was all a dream.

MATTHEW HARRISON (9)

Edge Hill Junior School, Burton-Upon-Trent

THE HUNTED

A ferocious tiger was asleep in a dark, gloomy cave.
Hunters spotted the tiger and tried to sneak up on
it. A hunter trod on a twig and woke the tiger up.
Suddenly the tiger chased them into a booby-trapped
forest and they were never heard of again.

JACK CADD (9)

Edge Hill Junior School, Burton-Upon-Trent

GRAVEYARD

I know I shouldn't be scared but I am. I got lost and it must be way past 5 o'clock. I got chased by the school bully. It's dark here so you can imagine how I feel. I take one step towards the gate, I try to lift one foot.

CHLOE MAYNE (9)
Edge Hill Junior School, Burton-Upon-Trent

THE GHOST

I walked through the dark dusty room, suddenly the television came on. My friend was scared. A ghost zipped out of the telly and flew into the ceiling. The ceiling crashed down and I just managed to escape but my best friend was never to be seen again.

MITCHELL WOODWARD (9)

Edge Hill Junior School, Burton-Upon-Trent

BRIAN AND THE ROTTEN APPLE

Sitting in his classroom, schoolboy Brian felt strange. The smell of a rotten apple was so tempting. Could he keep his secret? He could feel his disguise slipping. His human suit fell off, his wings flapped and he flew to the apple. Brian was really a giant fly! *Buzz buzz.*

GEORGE CHAMBERLAIN (9)
Edge Hill Junior School, Burton-Upon-Trent

INDIANA BLUE BEAR AND THE CURSE OF THE GOLDEN CAT

In the Sahara desert, Indiana Blue Bear and six of his men went to go and find the golden cat. They found a temple where, lying asleep was the golden cat. Indiana Blue Bear grabbed it and suddenly a huge boulder began to roll. What will Blue Bear do next?

ALEXANDER WEBSTER (9)

Edge Hill Junior School, Burton-Upon-Trent

THE MAGIC HEDGE

There was a gigantic hedge that opened when you touched the magic leaf. One little girl touched the leaf and the hedge opened. She skipped in and spotted a butterfly. She followed it and lost the gap. She decided to keep following the butterfly. I think she escaped, don't you?

MOLLY VECKUNGS (9)

Edge Hill Junior School, Burton-Upon-Trent

THE FLY

One day a giant fly started to attack the city but then the people started a plan to stop it. They put food on a giant flytrap. The fly fell straight into the trap and the city was saved. Suddenly Timmy awoke only to find this was all a nightmare.

JAMIE PEARSALL (9)

Edge Hill Junior School, Burton-Upon-Trent

THE DOG WHO TURNED INTO A BOY

One day the Walker family decided to go down to the field so they could give their dog some exercise. They threw the brand new ball and he caught it but ten seconds later, he turned into a boy. The Walker family were amazed, they loved the boy.

TILLY KING (9)
Edge Hill Junior School, Burton-Upon-Trent

THE DARKNESS

I started to climb the tower thinking, *got to run*.
The evil devils were chasing me yelling, 'Come back!'
but what I didn't notice was the passage was getting
darker and darker, the voices fainter and fainter.
Now I knew it was over. I was about to die. *Save me!*

DONTAE JONES (9)
Edge Hill Junior School, Burton-Upon-Trent

THE CAMPFIRE

The campfire was crackling, the wind howling.
The cubs were all nervously giggling, toasting soft
marshmallows. Eerie sounds and breaking twigs
were making them frightened. Was it a ghost? Or
even worse, a hungry wild animal? A shining light
appeared. A UFO! *Aliens!*
'Boo!' it's Akela! Or was it?

GEORGIA COLLYER (9)

Edge Hill Junior School, Burton-Upon-Trent

WHAT'S THERE?

I stood on a dark road. I was going home when
I heard a noise. I said, 'Who's there?'
Then I heard a creak; I was so terrified. It made me
jump up at least one foot in the air. I ran off, as fast as
my legs could go.

THOMAS CLORLEY (10)
Greenacres Primary School, Shrewsbury

THE WRIGGLING CHEST

I was going to see my friend to fetch the wriggling chest. I got there in one hour. Soon the chest would be gone. The desert was extremely hot, so I had to bury the chest fast. After the wriggling chest was buried, I told him and it was over.

SOPHIE BANKS (11)

Meadows Primary School, Telford

ADVENTURES OF JAMMIE

In a galaxy far away lived a green-eyed alien, he'd lost something really special. He looked in his house, his garden … then feeling a sharp poke in his pocket, he snatched it out and realised it was his special watch. That's what he was looking for. What a relief.

JAMIE SMITH (11)
Meadows Primary School, Telford

MYSTERY FOOTPRINTS

I was pushing through the long thick grass and getting as dirty as a mole. Suddenly I saw some large footprints. I moved closer, wanting to investigate. Still struggling through the thick, sticky mud, I did not give up. Then I peered around the thick oak tree.
Argh!

SHELLEY FERGUSSON (10)

Meadows Primary School, Telford

TERROR OF WICKED MANOR

The moon came up. Sam grabbed her flashlight and ran out of the house. Moments later she arrived at Wicked Manor, slowly she crept in. She heard a rusty cupboard open. All of a sudden, glasses started flying out of it, she spun around; one glass was flying towards her ...

PAIGE CRUISE (10)

Meadows Primary School, Telford

HUMPTY DUMPTY

As Humpty lay there, horses and king's men looking at him, he felt incomplete. 'Do I have something on my face?' he asked with a jittery voice. Suddenly Humpty heard a siren. It was an ambulance. Paramedics rushed over.
'You fell off a wall, don't worry you're in good hands!'

CHARLOTTE ADAMS (11)
Meadows Primary School, Telford

THE PIGEON THAT'S DYING

Misty came home on the verge of dying. It was a windy day and he had been blown into a wire. He had broken both of his legs, he could not stand up and blood was everywhere. He was a champion racing pigeon.

LUKE CADWALLADER (11)
Meadows Primary School, Telford

THE FINAL STAGE

'Eventually I made it,' said Lu' Kang as he entered into the dragon king's lair. He crossed the bridge into the arena on the other side of it. Lu' Kang saw Onagar dip his claws into the lava that was surrounding the arena. Onagar peered over his shoulder and he stood up.

HARRY JONES (11)

Meadows Primary School, Telford

THE ROBBERS

One day John called his friends and said, 'Come quick, robbers have got into my home.' When the friends arrived, they shouted, 'FBI give up.'
John came down the stairs and attacked the robbers, just as the real police arrived. Thanks to his friends, no one was hurt that day.

NATHAN CLARKE (10)

Our Lady & St Oswald's Catholic Primary School, Oswestry

MORRIS AND SWEETIE

One day in a small wooden cottage lived a small cute cat. The cat was named Morris, Morris was in the garden when he heard his friend Sweetie wanted Morris to come and share some of her biscuits. He was hungry, yum! Suddenly all of Sweetie's biscuits were absolutely *gone!*

NIAMH MAGUIRE (10)

Our Lady & St Oswald's Catholic Primary School, Oswestry

DEATH BAY

The ship arrived in Death Bay. The captain stepped out. He had been here before but never again! The chill told him something was wrong. Just then a speeding ghost appeared from the mist and went straight up his nostrils. Then the captain fell to his knees and screamed.

OLIVER RENWICK (10)

Our Lady & St Oswald's Catholic Primary School, Oswestry

ZAPPED UP

I went swimming in the sea, *happy as larry*, playing with my friends Alex and Zoe. Suddenly I saw a flash of light and we were zapped up by aliens. I was petrified. I often visit my friends the aliens but only at night when no one knows I'm missing.

ELIZABETH ROGERS-LEGGATT (9)
Our Lady & St Oswald's Catholic Primary School, Oswestry

HELP!

Thump, thump, thump! Was the noise of hundreds of elephants strolling past me, their smooth, dry skin rubbed my hands. The screech of the school bus deafened me, the elephants roared. There was a stampede of elephants and humans. Everything went wild, what was wrong? The herds rushed away. *Help!*

LAUREN CRANE (10)

Our Lady & St Oswald's Catholic Primary School, Oswestry

THE GALAXY TRAIN

Jake Johnson woke up and looked out of the window. He was in Planet Galaxy. He thought, *how am I going to get to school?* He then walked down the stairs and remembered the map of the galaxy. The map showed the flying trains, what great adventures might there be?

HANNAH SHEVLIN (9)

Our Lady & St Oswald's Catholic Primary School, Oswestry

62

MIDNIGHT TEDDIES

Just as midnight's striking, when everyone's asleep,
teddies yawn. Stretch, stretch, and out of warm beds
creep. They sneak out from their houses and creep
down the empty street, heading to the park.
Then behind the teddies, the owner Tom said, 'Let's
head home.'
'OK,' and they both fell asleep.

LUKE EVANS (9)

Our Lady & St Oswald's Catholic Primary School, Oswestry

OUR DAY TRIP TO PLANET EARTH

Dad always wanted to visit Earth, Dad didn't know
about the tall spiky things when we landed. While
Dad mended the undercarriage, I went exploring
and met an earthling with two eyes and two listening
organs. It made a horrible high-pitched noise and ran
… I hope we don't return.

SEBASTIAN BANKS (9)

Our Lady & St Oswald's Catholic Primary School, Oswestry

THE HOLIDAY

I waited in the car to go on holiday. I had nothing to do for hours. When I got there, the holiday home looked like it had not been cleaned for years. My mum got angry and walked straight out the door leaving me alone in the horrible house. *Sob!*

EMMA JONES (8)

Our Lady & St Oswald's Catholic Primary School, Oswestry

FLOPPY

One day there was a girl named Libby. Libby had a rabbit called Floppy. Floppy was a big brown rabbit, he loved playing and eating lots of carrots. Libby was playing outside when she saw a dog running after Floppy. She was scared! Would Floppy be OK? Libby began running.

LIBBY STOWELL (8)

Our Lady & St Oswald's Catholic Primary School, Oswestry

THE HOUSE OF DOOM

Emma and Immy entered a dark house. Above them lingered cobwebs and bats. They crept up the stairs and heard faint screams, so they walked towards the sound and found a skeleton with a white figure hovering above it. 'Argh!' screamed the girls and they ran out the crooked door.

AOIFE HOLBROOK (9)

Our Lady & St Oswald's Catholic Primary School, Oswestry

ALIEN

'Help! I surrender!' said a shopkeeper from across the road. *Crash, bang, wallop!* A spaceship crashed into the building and bits were flung into the air. When it had crashed onto the floor, a door opened and out came an alien. Someone found him and took him home.

TOBY CHUNSI (8)

Our Lady & St Oswald's Catholic Primary School, Oswestry

THE THING IN THE WOODS

After school, one sunny day, my mum told me we were going to an adventure park. 'Where's Dad?' I asked.
'Wait and see,' she said. When we arrived, we took a picnic to the woods. Suddenly a giant lizard jumped out, pulled off its skin, it was Dad in disguise!

ALEX DAVIES (9)

Our Lady & St Oswald's Catholic Primary School, Oswestry

THE HORROR HOUSE

One day there was a scary horror house. A girl called Annabel went into the scary horror house not knowing that it was a haunted house, so she opened the door and went in. The stairs creaked and she heard screaming, Annabel quickly ran away, not looking back.

BAILEY ROSS (8)

Our Lady & St Oswald's Catholic Primary School, Oswestry

EXPERIMENTER

There once lived a man who liked experimenting with potions. He was turning a white cat into an evil black pet. The experiment was a disaster, the evil potion changed the wicked man to kindness and caring. His potions helped turn others over the years from wickedness to kindness.

DEMELZA BROOKFIELD (10)

Our Lady & St Oswald's Catholic Primary School, Oswestry

THE SECRET CALL

One day a ginger cat named Tibs was playing in the garden when a group of mice came across the garden, he couldn't catch them so he made a secret sign and the cats came. When they caught them, they all had a big dinner feast, hooray! The cats won!

SUSAN MUNDAY (8)

Our Lady & St Oswald's Catholic Primary School, Oswestry

A MYSTERY TALE

The moon rose as I ran down the tremendously long path. My legs were trembling, my neck was sweating, I didn't know what to do! I had no idea what I was running from. The lamps in the street went out. I woke up to see it was a dream.

LIBBIE DAVIES (10)

Ridgeway Primary School, Burntwood

FINDING THE TREASURE

There I was looking for treasure but was there any hope? *No!* Digging for hours but suddenly, what was that? Something hard … then I dug as fast as I could and there it was - my own treasure chest.
I opened it, slowly piles of diamonds gleamed before my own eyes.

ELLIE BIRCH (10)

Ridgeway Primary School, Burntwood

M17'S SILLY SPACE

We landed. It was a strange start with Cyclops and
robots and a triangular boxing ring. There were
robots and what was that? It was slimy and very fat.
As I walked closer, I started to shake.
'Hello' I whispered.
'Booda.' He answered. Then I remembered M17's
space base!

TONY ALLSOPP (10)

Ridgeway Primary School, Burntwood

75

THE GHOSTS

The girl crept down the stairs and in the corner of her eye, suddenly she saw a ghost. She cried for help but they couldn't hear her. After a while, the ghost disappeared, then the girl went back to sleep but she knew that the ghost hadn't gone. *Oh no!*

JESSICA BIRCH (10)
Ridgeway Primary School, Burntwood

THE MYSTERIOUS FIGURE

I went to bed, it was freezing. The window was open. The curtains were flapping everywhere. I looked around, there on the door was a ghostly white figure, so as fast as I could, I turned on the lights but it was my dressing gown, what a relief.

OLIVIA PIKE (10)
Ridgeway Primary School, Burntwood

77

FAIRY DUST

One gloomy day there lived two fairies called Amy and Alice. They liked to play outside but bad things happened every week. One day they thought they should play, suddenly *bam,* they went to a parallel world. 'Oh no, where are we? Help! Help!' they started to shout.

CHLOE PEARCE (10)

Ridgeway Primary School, Burntwood

THE BUMPY JOURNEY

There was a boy called Tom. He went on holiday in a caravan. One night, a storm blew and the caravan got tipped over so he went to the nearest town to tell someone before the caravan blew into the river. The caravan got picked up and everyone was OK.

LAUREN YEOMANS (10)
Ridgeway Primary School, Burntwood

THE MAGIC HOLIDAY

There was a little girl called Alice, she went on holiday to Turkey. They went on an aeroplane, she flew at ten thirty at night, they got there at five o'clock am. They hired a car, they had two weeks there. When they got back, they were very brown.

SOPHIE MORRIS (10)

Ridgeway Primary School, Burntwood

LOCH NESS ... CHICKEN

'Out from nowhere comes the beast, devouring
anything in its path. First, revealing, the head, then
eyes, and last of all ... no one knows, the only person
not to be killed by it died of shock from the ghost of
the creature. But he rose from the dead
... And I'm him!

JAKE BAMFORD (10)

St Chad's CE (VE) Primary School, Lichfield

POP GOES THE GUM

Finally, he had it! Everlasting chewing gum! It could develop to be as voluminous as the world. Bob was gobbling his everlasting chewing gum. He blew it, the dimensions grew amazingly. Incredibly, after only five minutes, it took over the world.

KIERAN BROMLEY (10)
St Chad's CE (VE) Primary School, Lichfield

READY FOR A DUEL

As I flew into Kessel, the tension grew inside of me.
I knew one mistake and it was the end of me.
We landed, the doors opened, I slowly strolled
outside. It was quiet, too quiet. I hid behind a rock
but it wasn't a trap, I overreacted.
But suddenly …

JACK DAVEY (9)

St Chad's CE (VE) Primary School, Lichfield

JUNGLE OF DOOM

We ran as fast as cheetahs, followed by the tiger
licking its lips ready for dinner. Sara swung on a tatty
vine across the river, safe from the tiger. The other
vine snapped, I was devastated. No return!
Should I give up or run? *Argh!*

GEMMA HIGGS (10)
St Chad's CE (VE) Primary School, Lichfield

CHANGES

Everything has changed. Nothing's the same.
The small one is dead; thanks to Joe. But there's still
the mum to come. Nobody except for me and Joe
now. But we can't convince people to believe us!
As I look round at the despairing people, I wonder
what will happen next ...

LUCY COXON (10)
St Chad's CE (VE) Primary School, Lichfield

THE CRYSTAL STONE

I'd been digging for ages, I was bursting to find the crystal stone. My legs and arms were aching but I couldn't give up now. I was just bursting to find it. I carried on digging. Suddenly I hit something, could it be? 'Mum, I've hit something hard! Please be it …'

SARAH BRAMMER (10)
St Chad's CE (VE) Primary School, Lichfield

WHAT'S NEXT?

Suddenly I heard a peculiar movement coming from the cupboard. I crept up to it cautiously. My heart was pounding furiously. Suddenly my sister jumped out of the cupboard and shouted, 'Boo!'
'You didn't half make me jump! But don't worry, I'll get you back!' I warned.

LEWIS GARDNER (10)
St Chad's CE (VE) Primary School, Lichfield

87

SHEEP INVADER

Shaun had been acting in a very strange way lately. One night I was lying in my bed when I heard a *clank!* 'Oh no, Shaun was on the roof again,' I stepped outside and there was a blinding light. It was Shaun and an army of sheep invaders …

BEN EGGINTON (10)
St Chad's CE (VE) Primary School, Lichfield

WHO'S A CLEVER PARROT?

Clive and Clyde were brothers, they lived with their dad, Bob and Uncle John. One day John was found slumped against the wall. Bob asked himself, who would do this?

Suddenly Polly the parrot squawked
'Clyde don't, please!'
Bob grabbed Clyde.
'Clever Polly, you learn quickly,' whispered Clive.

ROSIE SHARP (10)
St Chad's CE (VE) Primary School, Lichfield

THE FLUFFY WHITE TAIL

The noise was overwhelming as I was bundled into the gate, I heard dogs whining … the gates opened. I was off! Driven on only by anger from the fluffy white tail bobbing up and down in front of me … I wish I wasn't a racing greyhound.

EMILY HOLMES (9)
St Chad's CE (VE) Primary School, Lichfield

DOOMSDAY!

One sweltering day in Mexico, Julio Ficardo walked into a radioactive pit, at the same time as a moth. There was a colossal bang and flash. The following day, a figure with yellow claws, red eyes and transparent moth-like wings, was seen on the bridge. *Disaster ...*

JEEVAN GARCHA (10)
St Chad's CE (VE) Primary School, Lichfield

THE ALIEN

Suddenly there was a blinding light out of the window, he ran to see what it was. He gazed up to find a UFO hovering above his back garden. He ran down the stairs as fast as his legs could take him, out of his back door to find …

THOMAS LOVELL (10)
St Chad's CE (VE) Primary School, Lichfield

THE WAR

As I sprinted for cover, I pulled out my machine gun and reloaded it. I could hear gunshots and bombs going off everywhere. I summoned up the courage, spun round and started firing. Suddenly something hit me, I fell to my knees in dismay. My eyes closed.

MATTHEW LOVELL (10)
St Chad's CE (VE) Primary School, Lichfield

93

THE BIGGEST SCARE IN THE SEA!

As I stood in the clean, tropical water, everything was prefect until … the ocean started rippling and the sight wasn't so pretty anymore. A gargantuan school of whales, sharks, dolphins and killer whales came crashing towards me. It was an accident waiting to happen!

HANNAH CLARK (10)

St Chad's CE (VE) Primary School, Lichfield

THE CHOPPING BLOCK OR A WIFE'S WORST NIGHTMARE

My heart was pumping, I was sweating, tears dripped down in torrents. Henry hadn't acknowledged my existence all day. I knew something was going to happen but what? I lay on the execution table, screamed for the last time and took my final breath.

OLIVIA RENUKA (10)

St Chad's CE (VE) Primary School, Lichfield

WHAT'S IT LIKE TO BE IN AFGHANISTAN?

The sun is beating on you, everywhere you go you can hear bullets firing, bombs going off. *Bang!* Also you will hear people dying everywhere. You are never alone or safe, not even the British Army can save you. It's the living hell. People are coming for you. Be safe!

STEVIE O'SULLIVAN (10)

St Chad's CE (VE) Primary School, Lichfield

THE BATTLE FOR PARIS

The doors opened ... my heart missed a beat,
my ears were ringing. I summoned up all my courage
and jumped. The sky turned into a fireball as the
plane took a direct hit. I was alone falling through the
sky, I pulled my ripcord, nothing happened. Then ...
oh dear ... *splat!*

BEN GREEN (10)
St Chad's CE (VE) Primary School, Lichfield

THE ENDLESS WAR

The Vastjanarader were catching up. 'You five get behind bunker!' *Boom!* The door went flying. 'Open fire!' *Zap!*

'Come on we need to get to the orb first.'

'Let's go soldiers so we can finish off the humans.' Echoed the terrorising voice of the Vastjanarader boss, 'Surrender or else!'

ALEX JONES (9)

St Chad's CE (VE) Primary School, Lichfield

THE HOUSE

A man was walking along the cold, wet sand. Then he was gone beneath the waves. An abandoned house was next to the sea, some kids went inside. Then the man came in the house, the kids were afraid but the scary man said, 'Hello kids.' It was Dad!

SAM TURNER (10)

St Chad's CE (VE) Primary School, Lichfield

THE CASTLE

The invasion of Warwick Castle commenced.
As the intruders descended, the soldiers frantically
sprinted to their action stations. While the king
ran wildly to safety, his soldiers fought to close the
gigantic drawbridge. Just in time, the bridge slammed
shut. Peace was restored.

TOM JOHNSON (10)
St Chad's CE (VE) Primary School, Lichfield

BACK IN TIME

It was dark and damp. There were cavemen all around. We'd gone back in time! 'Help!' I screamed. My heart was beating fast. I walked slowly forward. Suddenly the lights came on and I remembered I was in the London History Museum. I was so relieved. That was so realistic.

MEGAN CHAPLIN (8)

St Chad's CE (VE) Primary School, Lichfield

101

SCARED!

I was in a house with my friends and then something jumped out. All of us were scared. Then someone opened the creaky door, there were monsters of all sorts. But then everyone jumped out and said, 'Surprise, Happy Hallowe'en!' That night I had the best Hallowe'en of my life.

HANNAH GREEN (9)
St Chad's CE (VE) Primary School, Lichfield

THE DARK GHOST

I was sweating everywhere. I was alone on a wet, dark road. There was a funny noise, I went to see it, it was a ghost. I tried to make contact then suddenly it said, 'Hi, happy Hallowe'en!'
'Ah, it's Hallowe'en, I forgot, silly me, bye then and happy Hallowe'en!'

KIERON MACKENZIE (9)
St Chad's CE (VE) Primary School, Lichfield

COLOURFUL THING

There it is! Shimmering in the sky, what is it?
I wonder. Oh look it's coming down, it's orange, no
it's green, no red. Where is it now? Oh, there it is
on the field. Let's go have a look. Oh it's only my
brother's remote controlled plane. How silly!

LUCY FRYER (9)
St Chad's CE (VE) Primary School, Lichfield

THE BEAR ATTACK

I strolled into the cave terrified. I was alone except for some bats which kept flying around me hectically. My heart was pounding. *Argh!* A bear was attacking me. 'Help!' Phew it was only a nightmare. I grabbed my favourite teddy and cuddled it. Then my mum entered the room.

VICKY SMITH (9)
St Chad's CE (VE) Primary School, Lichfield

THE STRANGE CREATURE

I skipped along the path in the park, when suddenly a strange looking creature jumped right in front of me. It was green with yellow dots and had ten eyes. I squeaked 'Hello, my name is Daisy.
What is your name?' The creature did not answer. It quickly ran away.

CAMILLE MAUNAND (9)
St Chad's CE (VE) Primary School, Lichfield

THE BATTLE AGAINST SCARY MONSTERS

I was battling monsters. Then suddenly a ghost jumped out but I killed it. Then I shot a couple of zombies, obliterated a few vampires, then I went on the lifelike ghost train with Bob, (my cute, cuddly teddy, in my hand). I thought that ghost train was very scary!

FRASER SHANKLY (9)
St Chad's CE (VE) Primary School, Lichfield

BLACK AND WHITE

I was black, he was white. He moved, I moved.
I should never have done this, it was a big mistake.
He's coming and … check mate! I've never won this
before. I was losing and now I've won. I am the chess
champion of 2008!

SOPHIE CAPEWELL (9)
St Chad's CE (VE) Primary School, Lichfield

SURROUNDED

I was walking along a street and some monsters
jumped at me. My heart was pumping, I tried to run
through them but they scratched my leg. 'Argh!'
I shouted.
'Shh!' said a person behind me, those 3D gasses are
really realistic.

BEN CHURCHILL (9)
St Chad's CE (VE) Primary School, Lichfield

THE DINNER RACE

Wind rushed against the cheetah's fur, he was chasing a deer for dinner. The speed increased, his power developed. The deer was a small fragile thing, but big enough for his family of four. Suddenly he pounced, grasping the deer. Later on he arrived, his prize was taken, leaving bones.

ELLA STRAWBRIDGE (10)
Trefonen CE Primary School, Trefonen

CHILLY THE GIRAFFE

'How did that happen?' I asked, but I was too late, Chilly was my toy again. I'd gone to my friends, but they weren't my friends because when skating, they'd pushed me into ice but Chilly as a giraffe saved me. Then at home, he turned back into a toy.

ELLISSA HINGLEY (10)
Trefonen CE Primary School, Trefonen

TRAPPED

He was trapped. There was no way out. All he could hear was whispering getting closer. He could feel the crooked floor shaking beneath him. His heart pounded. The floor shook. The whispering got closer. Suddenly the door creaked open. They stood there staring. No one heard his screams. *Help!*

GRACE GRIFFITH (11)
Trefonen CE Primary School, Trefonen

JIMBO THE JUNGLE EXPLORER AND THE GOLDEN CUSTARD CREAM

Once in Jingly Jungle, Jimbo the jungle explorer had found the 'Golden Custard Cream!' He had run, swam and swung to get to it. Suddenly he noticed Timmy Tiger guarding it. Jimbo threw elephant dung at him, stole the creamy substance and ran! He was the best explorer ever!

HENRY LISTON (10)

Trefonen CE Primary School, Trefonen

SCHOOL TERROR ...

Norbert turned, he fell down a porthole of oxygen-less disbelief, the ground was close. He felt cold, the evil was stood behind him. His lips were grey as if all his blood was lost! He shook like an earthquake. It was ... the teacher holding his school report ...

NATALIE ROSE (11)
Trefonen CE Primary School, Trefonen

THE FAB HOLIDAY IN FRANCE

I'm going on a ferry to France. I've never been on a ferry before. I'm really, really, really excited. I really, really want a croissant. Can't forget the baguettes. I hope there's swimming pools. Oh no, it's over. No more croissants or baguettes or swimming pools. Time to go home.

HARRY STOKES (8)
Wigmore Primary School, Wigmore

IT WILL BE FUN IN ANGLESEY

Swimming in the sea at Anglesey - I like doing that.
I'm taking my caravan and my family and my sister.
I will be going to Home Farm Caravan Site to stay for
my holiday. It will be fun. I'll play in the playroom.
I will pay for sweets. Cool!

JAYDON BURNLEY (8)
Wigmore Primary School, Wigmore

AN ADVENTUROUS HOLIDAY

I'm really excited to go on my holiday. I am going in
a plane to fly to the jungle to see the monkeys with
their long tails. I hope it will be warm so we can see
the wonderful waterfalls and the monkeys playing
and eating. I am very excited.

REEVE JONES (9)

Wigmore Primary School, Wigmore

THE PLANE HOLIDAY

I'm going on a plane to Portugal. I'm staying in a hotel called Dom Pedro Golf. We are staying there for a week. Our room number is 821, we're going swimming in the sea and the pool. I can eat as much as I want. Downstairs there is air hockey.

BEN JONES (8)
Wigmore Primary School, Wigmore

A PARADISE IN SPAIN

I'm going on my holiday and I'm very, very excited. I'm going to Spain, very hot Spain. I'm definitely packing suncream and sunglasses. Luckily, I'm going on an aeroplane. First I'm going to the beach with a picnic. Then the pools, the freezing cold pools. Then we go home, boo!

MATTHEW OWEN (8)

Wigmore Primary School, Wigmore

FUN FAB HOLIDAY

On my holiday, I'm going to Blackpool. I'm going to splash about in the deep blue sea and go on all the rides. See all the ice-skating, go on Noah's Ark, go to the arcades and come back late at night.

NATASHA EVANS (8)

Wigmore Primary School, Wigmore

ADVENTUROUS

I am going to play outside with my rabbit.
My brother's kicking his ball. I like to watch him
playing with his football. I like to run with my brother
and play on my bike. I think it's very good fun to play.
I like to swim in my pool.

ANITA STEVENS (8)
Wigmore Primary School, Wigmore

LAST SUMMER

Last summer, I went to Disneyland Paris, I went on the huge roller coaster, then I went on the high water slide. *Splish, splash, splosh.* I had a cool chocolate and vanilla ice cream, *yum!* Next, I went on the twister ride, it made me feel sick!

OWEN BLACKBURNE (8)

Wigmore Primary School, Wigmore

A RELAXING HOLIDAY IN FRANCE

I'm going on a giant massive ferry to France soon, we'll go swimming in the pool, dining in the restaurant. I can look at the sea, the flowing blue sea. I'm taking my dog, my caravan and my family. It's the last day of my holiday, back home now. *Boo!*

KIERAN HARRIS (9)
Wigmore Primary School, Wigmore

LAST SUMMER

Last summer, I went on a massive boat with my family. We sailed around the hot sandy bay and went to see the seals. They stared at me as they swam alongside the boat. The seals were grey and lovely. It was fun. I wish I could go again.

ARRON MCLOUGHLIN (8)
Wigmore Primary School, Wigmore

INFORMATION

We hope you have enjoyed reading this book - and that you will continue to enjoy it in the coming years.

If you like reading and writing, drop us a line or give us a call and we'll send you a free information pack. Alternatively visit our website at www.youngwriters.co.uk

Write to:
Young Writers Information,
Remus House,
Coltsfoot Drive,
Peterborough,
PE2 9JX

Tel: (01733) 890066
Email: youngwriters@forwardpress.co.uk